HANSEL  AND GRETEL

Based on the tale by the Brothers Grimm

IAN WALLACE

Douglas & McIntyre   A GROUNDWOOD BOOK   Toronto Vancouver Buffalo

To Blair, June, Connor,
Trent and Janis
and, of course,
to Owen

Copyright © 1994 by Ian Wallace
Reprinted 1996
All rights reserved. No part of this book may be reproduced, stored in a
retrieval system or transmitted in any form or by any means, without the prior
written permission of the publisher, or in the case of photocopying or other
reprographic copying, a licence from CANCOPY (Canadian Reprography
Collective), Toronto, Ontario.

Groundwood Books/Douglas & McIntyre
585 Bloor Street West
Toronto, Ontario M6G 1K5

Distributed in the U.S. by Publishers Group West
4065 Hollis Street
Emeryville, CA 94608

The publisher gratefully acknowledges the assistance of the Canada Council, the Ontario Arts
Council and the Ontario Ministry of Culture, Tourism and Recreation.

Library of Congress Data is available.

Canadian Cataloguing in Publication Data

Main entry under title:
Hansel and Gretel
ISBN 0-88899-212-2
1. Fairy tales. 2. Folklore - Germany.
I. Wallace, Ian, 1950-

PZ8.Ha 1994   j398.21   C94-930727-0

Design by Michael Solomon
Illustrations rendered in pastel pencil on black Lana Balkis paper.
Printed and bound in Hong Kong by Everbest Printing Co. Ltd.

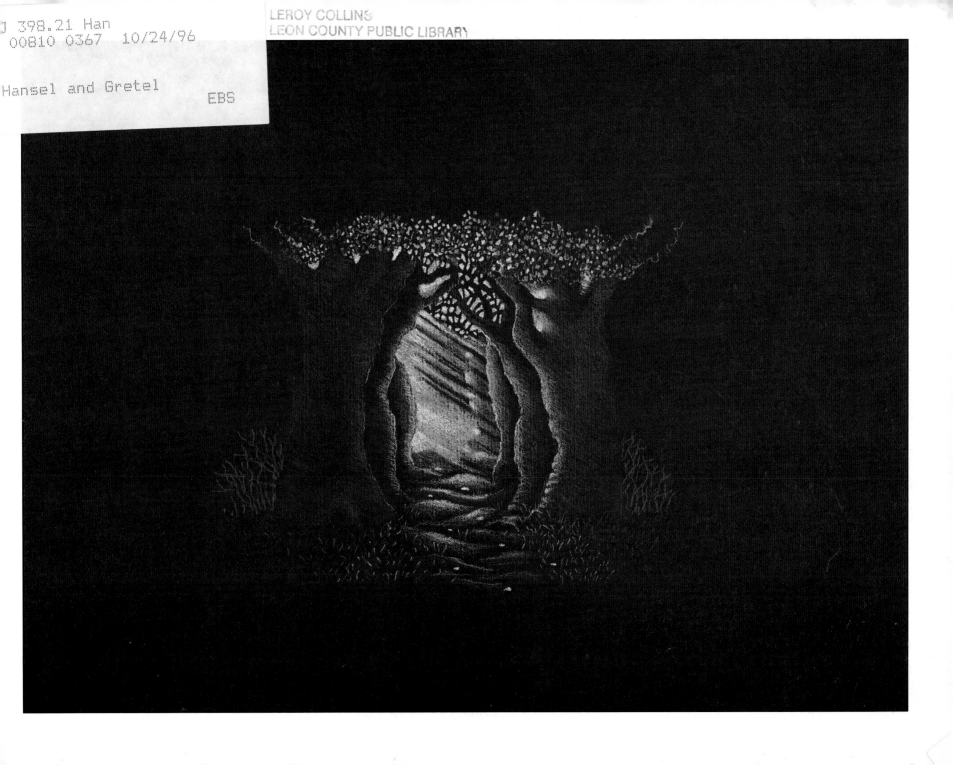

In a house by the sea on the edge of a large forest lived a poor fisherman with his wife and two children. The boy's name was Hansel and the girl was called Gretel. Times were hard, and soon the day came when the family could not even afford to buy food.

That night, the fisherman tossed and turned as he lay in bed.

"What is going to become of us?" he groaned to his wife. "How can we feed the children when we don't even have enough for ourselves?"

"There's only one thing to do," she answered. "Tomorrow morning we'll take the children with us when we go to cut wood. Then we'll leave them in the forest. They'll never find their way back, and we'll be rid of them."

"I can't just leave my children in the woods," the man cried. "They'll starve to death, if the wild animals don't tear them to pieces first."

"If we don't do something, all four of us will starve, and you might as well start building our coffins right now!" And she pestered the man until he finally agreed to do what she wanted.

In the next room, Hansel and Gretel lay awake, too hungry to sleep, and they overheard their parents talking.

"What are we going to do?" Gretel whispered.

"Don't worry," Hansel said. "I'll think of some way out of this."

Late that night, after their parents had fallen asleep, Hansel crept outside. Under the bright moonlight, white pebbles glistened on the ground like silver coins. Hansel quickly stuffed his pockets with as many pebbles as he could. Then he slipped back into the house and crawled into bed.

Early the next morning, the woman woke up the two children.

"Get up, you lazy things! You're coming with us to cut wood." She handed them each a piece of bread. "Here's your lunch. Don't eat it too soon, because this is all you're going to get today." Then they set off for the forest.

After they had walked awhile, Hansel and Gretel stopped and looked back at the house. They did this again and again until their father said, "What are you looking at? Stop dawdling and hurry up!"

"We're waving goodbye to the cat. She's sitting on the roof of the house."

"You fools," said the woman. "That's not the cat. It's just the morning sun shining on the chimney."

But the children had not been looking at the cat at all. Instead, they had been taking pebbles from their pockets and dropping them on the ground each time they stopped.

When they reached a spot in the middle of the forest, the woman said to the children, "Get a move on and build yourselves a fire. You'll stay here while we cut wood. When we've finished, we'll come back and get you."

So Hansel and Gretel gathered some twigs and brush and built themselves a fine fire. When noon came, they ate their bread. Then they sat and waited and waited, until finally their eyes closed, and they fell asleep.

When they woke up, the forest was pitch black, and there was no sign of their parents anywhere.

"What will we do now?" Gretel asked. "We'll never find our way home."

"Just wait a little while," her brother answered. "Wait until the moon rises."

Sure enough, when the full moon had risen, Hansel found the trail of white pebbles, gleaming like new coins, and the children followed them home.

When they finally arrived at the house, the woman opened the door.

"Where on earth have you two been?" she said crossly. "We thought you were never coming home!" Their father, however, was relieved and happy to see them, because he had felt terrible about abandoning them in the forest.

The next night, Hansel and Gretel overheard their parents talking again.

"We'll just have to try one more time," the woman said. "Tomorrow we'll take the children even farther into the forest so they'll never be able to find their way home. It's the only thing we can do."

The father thought it would be better for them all to starve together than abandon the children, but the woman would not listen. She just scolded, and because he had already given in to her once, in the end he agreed to her plan yet again.

Late in the night, Hansel got up to gather more pebbles. But the woman had locked the door, and he could not get out.

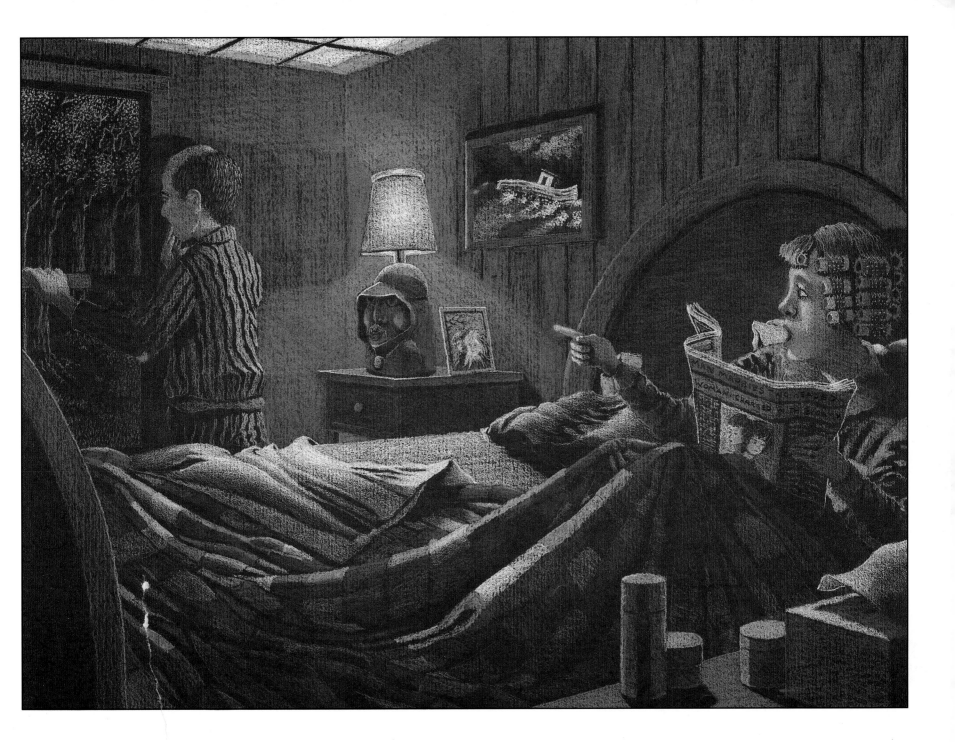

In the morning the woman gave each of the children another piece of bread, and this time she led the way, taking them even deeper into the forest. Their father, who was very unhappy, followed far behind.

As they walked, Hansel crumbled his bread in his pocket. Whenever he could, he stopped to throw a crumb on the ground.

"Hansel, what are you looking at?" asked the woman. "Have you forgotten how to use your legs?"

"I'm just waving goodbye to the pigeon. She's sitting on the roof of our house."

"You fool," said the woman. "That's not the pigeon. It's the morning sun shining on the chimney."

But little by little, Hansel managed to drop all the breadcrumbs onto the ground.

When they were in the thickest part of the forest, the children made another fire, and the woman said, "Now you two just rest here. We're going to chop wood, and when we've finished, we'll come back and get you."

When noon came, Gretel shared her bread with her brother. Then they fell asleep, and when they woke up, the forest was dark once again.

"Don't worry, Gretel," Hansel said. "Just wait until the moon rises. Then we'll see the crumbs I dropped, and they'll show us the way home."

But when the moon rose, there were no breadcrumbs, for the thousands of birds in the forest had picked them up and eaten them.

For the entire night and all the next day, the children wandered through the woods, but still they could not find their way home. Finally, so tired and hungry that their legs would no longer carry them, they lay down beneath a tree and fell asleep.

The next morning Hansel and Gretel began walking again. As they walked, the forest grew very black and quiet, and the trees seemed to close in behind them. The children knew that if they did not reach help soon, they would die of hunger and weariness.

Then, at noon, they saw a snow-white bird sitting on a branch. It sang so beautifully in the still forest that they stopped to listen. When the bird had finished its song, it spread its wings and fluttered ahead of them, and Hansel and Gretel followed.

Before long, they came to a small clearing, and in the middle of the clearing was a house. As the children drew closer, they could see that it was made of sweets, with a roof made of cake and pure sugar for windows.

"Gretel, look at that!" Hansel said. "I'm going to eat a piece of the roof. You can have some of the window."

He reached up and broke off a piece of cake, and Gretel pushed out a bit of windowpane and munched on it happily.

All at once they heard a voice calling from inside the house:

"Nibbling, nibbling like a mouse.
Who's that nibbling at my house?"

The door opened, and a very old woman came out, leaning on a cane. Hansel and Gretel were so frightened that they dropped what they had in their hands. But the woman just nodded and said, "Hello, my dears. What has brought you here? Come inside. You'll be safe with me."

She took them by the hand and led them into the house. Then she served them a huge meal of milk and pancakes with sugar and apples and nuts. Afterwards she made up two little beds with clean white sheets, and Hansel and Gretel fell into them and thought they were in heaven.

But the old woman was only pretending to be friendly. She was a wicked witch who had bewitched the forest and built her house to trap unsuspecting children. Whenever she managed to lure them into her clutches, she would cook them and eat them for a grand feast.

Early the next morning, the witch seized the sleeping Hansel and threw him into a pen. Then she poked Gretel awake. "Get up, you lazy thing, and cook your brother something tasty. We're going to fatten him up and then," she said. "I'm going to eat him."

Gretel had no choice. She had to obey the witch's orders.

So the very best food was cooked for poor Hansel, while Gretel got nothing to eat but crab shells.

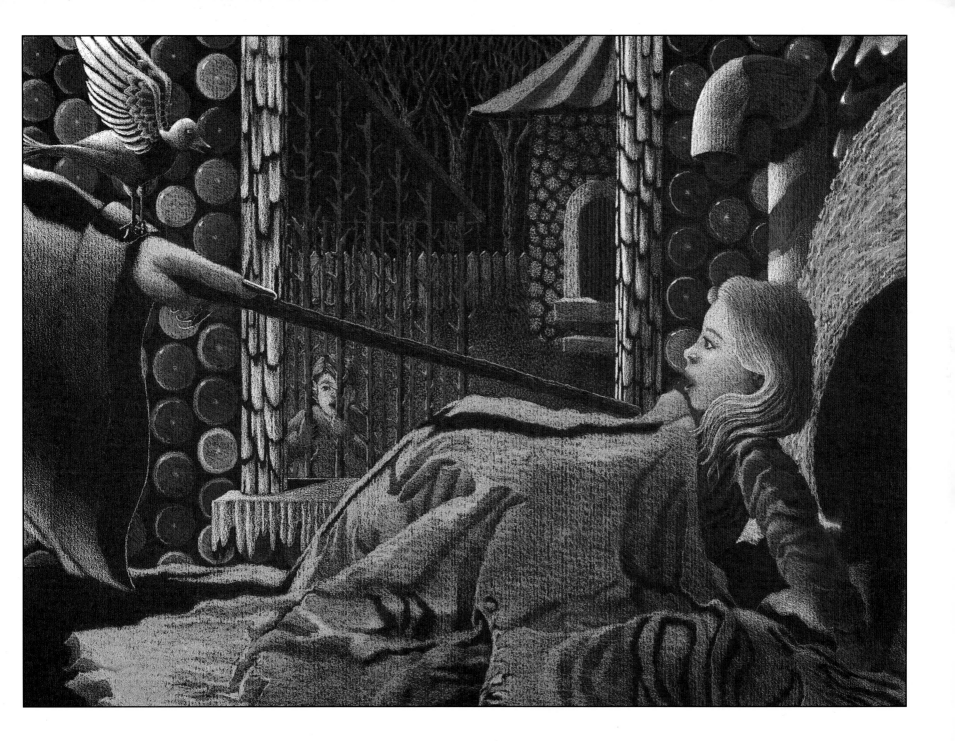

Every morning, the woman hobbled out to the cage and called out, "Hansel, stick out your finger so I can feel how fat you are." The witch had extremely poor eyesight, and she could not see very far. So Hansel stuck out a thin little bone, and the woman was fooled into thinking it was his finger.

Weeks went by, but still Hansel did not seem to get fat. Finally the witch decided not to wait any longer.

"Get a move on," she called to Gretel, "and fetch some water to fill the kettle. I don't care how thin he is. Tomorrow I'm going to cook him anyway."

With a heavy heart, Gretel did as she was told. "It would have been better to have been eaten by wild beasts in the forest," she said to her brother. "At least we could have died together!"

The next day, Gretel hung the kettle over the fire.

"First we'll bake," the old woman ordered. "I've already heated the oven. I want you to crawl inside to see if it's hot enough. Then we'll put the bread in." The witch planned to close the oven door once Gretel had climbed inside, for she wanted to roast and eat her, too.

"But I don't know how to do it," Gretel said, thinking quickly. "How do I get in?"

"You fool," cried the woman. "Watch me!" And she waddled up to the oven and stuck her head in the door.

Instantly, Gretel gave the witch a huge push that sent her head-first into the oven. Then she banged the door shut and bolted it.

The witch began to howl and scream, and soon she was miserably burned to death.

Gretel ran straight to her brother and unlocked the pen. "Hansel, we're saved! The witch is dead!" Hansel sprang out like a bird from a cage, and the two children hugged each other and danced for joy.

Inside the witch's house, they found chests filled with pearls and jewels.

"These are much better than pebbles," said Hansel. "But we'd better be off if we're going to find our way out of this forest."

So the children filled their pockets with as many jewels as they could hold, and they left the witch's house forever.

Outside the forest stirred in the early winter air, and the trees seemed to give way as the children walked. Gradually the forest began to look more and more familiar.

"What's that smell?" Gretel said, sniffing the air.

"It's the sea!" Hansel shouted.

Then, in the distance, they caught sight of their house. On the doorstep sat their father with his head in his hands. When he heard the children's voices, he looked up, and he began to run to them.

Hansel and Gretel threw their arms around their father's neck. The man had not had a single happy moment since he had abandoned his children in the forest, and in the meantime, his wife had died.

Hansel and Gretel emptied their pockets and showed their father their handfuls of pearls and jewels. Their troubles, at last, were over, and they lived together in perfect happiness from then on.